Make friends with

Sheltie

The little pony with the big heart

Sheltie is the lovable little Shetland pony with a big personality. His best friend and owner is Emma, and together they have lots of exciting adventures.

Share Sheltie and Emma's adventures in

SHELTIE THE SHETLAND PONY
SHELTIE SAVES THE DAY
SHELTIE AND THE RUNAWAY
SHELTIE FINDS A FRIEND
SHELTIE TO THE RESCUE
SHELTIE IN DANGER
SHELTIE RIDES TO WIN
SHELTIE AND THE SADDLE MYSTERY
SHELTIE LEADS THE WAY
SHELTIE THE HERO
SHELTIE AND THE STRAY

Peter Clover was born and went to school in London. He was a storyboard artist and illustrator before he began to put words to his pictures. He enjoys painting, travelling, cooking and keeping fit, and lives on the coast in Somerset.

Also by Peter Clover in Puffin

The Sheltie Series

Sheltie in Trouble

Peter Clover

PUFFIN BOOKS

For Stephen Gregory Blue

PUFFIN BOOKS

Published by the Penguin Group
Penguin Books Ltd, 80 Strand, London WC2R 0RL, England
Penguin Putnam Inc., 375 Hudson Street, New York, New York 10014, USA
Penguin Books Australia Ltd, Ringwood, Victoria, Australia
Penguin Books Canada Ltd, 10 Alcorn Avenue, Toronto, Ontario, Canada M4V 3B2
Penguin Books India (P) Ltd, 11 Community Centre, Panchsheel Park, New Delhi – 110 017, India
Penguin Books (NZ) Ltd, Cnr Rosedale and Airborne Roads, Albany, Auckland, New Zealand
Penguin Books (South Africa) (Pty) Ltd, 24 Sturdee Avenue, Rosebank 2196 South Africa

Penguin Books Ltd, Registered Offices: 80 Strand, London WC2R 0RL, England

www.penguin.com

First published 1998
7

Copyright © Working Partners Ltd, 1998
All rights reserved

Created by Working Partners Ltd, London W12 7QY

The moral right of the author/illustrator has been asserted

Filmset in 14/20 Palatino

Made and printed in England by Clays Ltd, St Ives plc

Except in the United States of America, this book is sold subject to the condition that it shall not, by
way of trade or otherwise, be lent, re-sold, hired out, or otherwise
circulated without the publisher's prior consent in any form of binding or cover other than that in
which it is published and without a similar condition including this
condition being imposed on the subsequent purchaser

British Library Cataloguing in Publication Data
A CIP catalogue record for this book is available from the British Library

ISBN 0-141-30136-8

Chapter One

Emma had just got home from school.
And the first thing she always did
after school was rush out to the
paddock to see Sheltie, her little
Shetland pony.

As usual, Sheltie was standing by
the gate, waiting for her. He tossed his
head and gave a shrill whinny. That
was Sheltie's way of saying hello.

Emma patted and hugged the little

pony. Then she gave him a good rub
behind the ears as Sheltie nuzzled her
shirt pocket looking for his carrot.
Every day, Emma took a carrot to
school with her in her book bag. And
she always had it ready in her pocket
for Sheltie as a treat the moment she
came home.

While Sheltie munched on his carrot
Emma noticed that he was standing on
three legs and holding up his left leg
so that only the tip of his hoof was
touching the ground. There was
something wrong with his left foreleg.

'What's the matter, boy?' asked
Emma. 'Have you got a stone in your
shoe?'

Sheltie blew a snort and shuffled
uncomfortably.

'I won't be a minute,' said Emma. 'I'll just go and get changed and then I'll take a look at it for you.'

She hurried inside to put on her jeans and a T-shirt.

Mum came out of the cottage with Joshua while Emma went to the tack room to fetch Sheltie's hoof pick.

'Poor Sheltie,' said Joshua.

Mum watched Emma as she picked up Sheltie's left leg and felt under his shoe with her finger.

'There doesn't seem to be anything here,' said Emma. She put his hoof down.

'Check his lower leg,' said Mum.

Emma ran her hand gently down Sheltie's left leg. Then she felt his right leg. The left one was definitely larger.

'It's swollen,' said Emma. 'What do you think we should do, Mum?'

'Maybe Sheltie has twisted his leg in a hole or something,' suggested Mum.

Emma knew that there were a lot of things that could make a pony lame. Some of them could just be a nuisance, like a simple sprain. Others could be quite serious.

'I think we should get the vet to come along to see him,' added Mum. 'Just to be on the safe side.' Then she went inside to telephone Mr Thorne, leaving Joshua with a very worried Emma.

Mum came out again quite quickly.

'Emma,' she called as she hurried down the garden, 'we're in luck. Mr Thorne's up at the farm looking at Mr

4

Brown's sick cow. He said he'd pop in when he passes by in about fifteen minutes.'

Emma brightened a little. She hugged Sheltie and pressed her cheek against his neck. 'Poor Sheltie,' she whispered. 'Does it hurt, boy?'

'He seems cheerful enough,' said Mum. 'Let's hope it's nothing serious!'

Sheltie was actually quite enjoying all the attention. He raised his sore hoof off the ground and looked up at Emma as if to say, 'I've got a bad leg.'

When Mr Thorne arrived he checked Sheltie over and said that it was nothing more than a slight sprain.

'Sheltie's leg will need a bandage for support though,' he added. 'And he should only have light exercise for a day or two. You mustn't ride him until the swelling goes down, Emma.'

Emma knew that things like this sometimes happened to ponies. And she knew that you had to be patient or things could get worse. Emma wasn't normally very good at waiting. But where Sheltie was concerned she could always be patient. And the vet promised that Sheltie's leg would be as good as new in a couple of days.

Mr Thorne took a thick crêpe bandage out of his bag and showed Emma how to wrap it tightly around Sheltie's left leg. Emma concentrated really hard. Sheltie stood absolutely still while the vet tied the bandage.

'There! All done,' said Mr Thorne. 'Do you think you can do this again tomorrow, Emma? The bandage will probably work a bit loose during the day, so you will have to wrap it again.'

'I think I can,' said Emma. 'But will you help me, Mum, in case I do it wrong?'

'Of course I will,' said Mum. 'Don't worry, Emma. We'll all look after Sheltie.'

Chapter Two

With the bandage on his leg, Sheltie
was able to stand properly on all
fours. 'It's not as bad as it seems,
Emma,' said Mr Thorne. 'It's just like
when you twist your ankle.'

Emma knew what that felt like. She
had twisted her own ankle once, at
school.

The next morning when Emma gave

Sheltie his breakfast he seemed a lot better. And that afternoon when she came home from school, the first thing Emma did was to check Sheltie's bandage.

Just like Mr Thorne had said, the bandage had worked itself loose during the day, and it was all wrinkled.

Emma called Mum, then set about rebandaging Sheltie's leg. It didn't seem to be so swollen now and Emma was really pleased. She even managed to wrap Sheltie's leg perfectly on her own.

'Well done, Emma,' smiled Mum. 'You didn't need my help after all, did you?'

'I think I'll give Sheltie a groom,'

said Emma. 'Then I'll take him out for some light exercise. A nice walk on his lead rein. You'll like that, won't you, Sheltie?'

Sheltie answered with a soft whinny as Emma dashed off to the tack room to fetch his combs and brushes.

After half an hour of brushing, Emma exclaimed, 'Sheltie, I don't think your coat has ever looked so bright and shiny!' Sheltie's light-chestnut coat gleamed in the late afternoon sunshine.

The little Shetland pony looked back over his shoulder and squinted at Emma through his big brown eyes. This made Emma giggle. 'You'll probably need sunglasses now,' she said.

Sheltie blew a raspberry then turned his attention back to a clump of dandelions he had discovered and continued munching away happily.

'How about a nice gentle walk, Sheltie?' said Emma.

Sheltie blew another snort. He didn't know exactly what Emma had said. But he knew enough to know that it was time to be taken out.

Sheltie flicked his tail and stood very still while Emma slipped on his head collar.

But as Emma bent down to pick up the brushes and put them away before they set off, Sheltie decided to have some fun. It was too much for the little pony to resist. He pushed Emma with

a playful nudge and sent her headlong
into the long grass.

'Sheltie!' giggled Emma. But her
playful pony had already escaped to
the other side of the paddock and was
waiting for Emma to chase him.

'Come here, Sheltie!' said Emma.
She was trying to sound stern. 'You're
not supposed to be rushing around

like that.' Sheltie lowered his head and raised his bandaged leg.

'Yes, that's right,' said Emma. 'You're supposed to be taking things nice and easy.'

Sheltie walked over and gently nuzzled her arm. Emma wasn't really cross. She was only pretending. Although he was a pony and not a person, Sheltie was Emma's very best friend.

Emma's best human friend was Sally, who lived near by in Fox Hall Manor.

Sally had a pony called Minnow, and the two girls often went riding together. But for the next two weeks Emma and Sheltie would have to go out on their own. Sally was away on holiday with her parents in Scotland. And Minnow was being stabled at the riding school until they returned.

'It's a pity that Sally and Minnow aren't here to see how neat and tidy you are, isn't it, Sheltie?' said Emma.

Sheltie peered through his floppy forelock with such an appealing look that Emma suddenly had a brilliant idea.

'I'm going to take your picture,' she said, 'and send it to Sally in Scotland. After all, it's not every day that you look like a film-star pony, is it?'

Sheltie tossed his freshly brushed mane.

'Now, you stand there and be a good boy while I go and fetch Dad's camera.'

Sheltie did as he was told and stood
with his fuzzy chin resting on the top
bar of the wooden fence. He waited
patiently and watched Emma as she
ran up the garden to the cottage.

But when Emma came out again
with the camera, Sheltie was practising
one of his favourite pastimes – rolling.
Sheltie was having a dust-bath in the
dry earth by the paddock gate. A big

cloud of grey dust puffed up around him as he rolled and snorted happily.

'Oh no!' cried Emma. 'All that hard work!' But she couldn't stop laughing all the same. Sheltie looked so funny lying on his back with all four legs kicking up in the air. And she was pleased that he was feeling a little better. Sheltie's sore leg didn't seem to be bothering him much at all.

It wasn't quite the photograph that Emma had hoped for, but she took a snap all the same.

'I bet that will make a smashing photo!' said a voice suddenly, out of nowhere.

Emma was taken completely by surprise and spun round so fast that she almost dropped the camera.

Chapter Three

A boy of Emma's age with dark curly hair and a big friendly grin stood only two metres away. He was wearing cotton shorts and a floppy T-shirt. Emma had never seen him before.

'Hello. My name's Gregory,' said the boy. 'Gregory Blue. Is that your pony?'

Gregory Blue was not at all shy. And he was full of questions. Even before Emma had answered his first question he had already asked another four.

'What kind of a pony is he? What's his name? Where does he live? And what's wrong with his leg?'

Emma started to laugh. She didn't mean to be rude. She simply wasn't sure if Gregory was being really friendly or just really nosy.

Now Gregory was standing on the bottom rail of the fence and leaning right over into the paddock.

Sheltie rolled himself up on to his feet and gave himself a good shake. Sheltie covered Gregory in dust and made himself sneeze.

Gregory sneezed too, then laughed and said, 'He's not very big, is he?'

'He's a Shetland pony,' said Emma. 'He's supposed to be small. But

19

actually,' she added, 'he's quite big for a Shetland. And his name is Sheltie.' Emma thought for a moment and wondered if she had answered all of Gregory's questions.

'Oh . . . and he belongs to me, he lives here in this paddock and he's got a sprained ankle.' There! Emma had answered the lot.

Gregory Blue smiled and rubbed Sheltie's head between his ears. 'He's a smasher, isn't he?'

Emma found herself smiling back. Even though he asked a lot of questions, there was something about Gregory Blue that made Emma like him straight away.

'Where did you come from anyway?' asked Emma. It was her turn to ask the questions now. 'Are you visiting Little Applewood? Where are you staying?'

Sheltie pushed his nose between the fence bars and nuzzled the pocket of

Gregory's shorts, looking for a peppermint.

'I'm on holiday,' laughed Gregory. 'We're staying in Stepps Cottage, at the end of the lane. I got bored indoors, so I came out for a walk. Then I saw you and Sheltie and I just had to come over to say hello.'

That was nice, thought Emma.

'I'd better be getting back now though,' said Gregory. 'I expect my mother will be wondering where I've got to.'

'I'll walk Sheltie down the lane with you,' said Emma. 'We're going that way, aren't we, boy?'

Sheltie blew through his lips and flicked his tail.

'Can't you ride him?' asked Gregory.

Emma explained why she couldn't ride Sheltie for a day or two. Then she clipped Sheltie's lead rein to his head collar and unlocked the paddock gate.

'When he's better,' said Gregory, 'will you let me have a ride?'

'I might,' smiled Emma. 'We'll see!'

'Thanks,' said Gregory. 'I hope we can be friends.'

Emma closed the gate and led Sheltie out into the lane.

At the end of the lane, Emma and Sheltie said goodbye to Gregory. They watched as he bounded up the steep flight of stone steps outside the cottage and turned at the front door.

'Can I come and see you and Sheltie tomorrow?' he yelled.

The next day was Saturday, so

Emma smiled and said cheerfully, 'If you like.' Emma thought it would be nice to have someone to play with while Sally was away. But she didn't realize how much of a handful Gregory Blue was going to be.

Chapter Four

The next morning, Gregory came to Emma's cottage early. Everyone was still sitting at the kitchen table having breakfast when they were interrupted by a loud knock at the back door.

'Who could that be?' said Mum. 'We're not expecting anyone, are we?' She opened the door and in walked Gregory.

'Hello,' he said brightly. 'My name's

Gregory and my mother said it's all right if I spend the day with you. She's going shopping in town and won't be back until four.'

'Emma!' Mum raised her eyebrows and looked from Gregory to Dad and then back to Emma. 'You didn't tell us you had invited anyone for the day!'

Emma felt her face turn red.

'I didn't,' she whispered. 'I only said he could come over to say hello to Sheltie.'

Dad looked at Gregory. And Gregory gave Dad a nice big smile.

'It is all right, isn't it?' said Gregory. 'I mean, if I stay?'

Dad couldn't help but smile. Gregory was cheeky, but he was so nice and friendly.

'I expect so,' answered Dad. 'Will that be all right?' he asked Mum.

'Of course it will,' she said. 'As long as your mother knows you're here, Gregory. Shall I give her a ring and tell her we're happy for you to stay?'

'No,' said Gregory. 'Anyway, she'll have gone out by now.'

Mum looked concerned. She wasn't sure if she believed him. 'Well, come and sit down, Gregory. Would you like some toast?'

'Yes, please,' said Gregory.

Emma watched him eat six slices.

'Didn't you have any breakfast this morning?' she asked.

'Only some cereal,' said Gregory. 'Mum was in a hurry.'

'And you're sure your mother

27

knows where you are?' asked Dad.

'Oh yes,' chirped Gregory. 'She was really pleased to get rid of me for the day.'

Mum gave Dad a quirky smile. 'I think we've got our hands full here,' she said to him.

'You can help me give Sheltie his breakfast afterwards, Gregory,' said Emma. 'I always have mine first on Saturdays!'

'I've already given him a little snack,' said Gregory. 'I hope you don't mind. I've given him some nice apples.'

Emma did mind. But she tried not to show it. Emma liked to feed Sheltie herself.

'How many apples did you give

him?' asked Emma. 'Sheltie's not supposed to have too many titbits. It's not good for him!'

Gregory looked embarrassed.

'How many apples, Gregory?' asked Mum.

Again, Gregory looked uncomfortable. 'Three, I think,' he said finally.

'Are you sure?' said Emma. She didn't think that Gregory was telling the whole truth.

'Yes, it was three. Three tiny little apples.' Gregory seemed pleased with his answer.

'And where did you get these three tiny apples from?' asked Dad. 'Did your mother give them to you?'

'Oh no,' said Gregory with a big grin. 'There's an old man who has apple trees, halfway up the lane. I asked him if I could have some apples for Sheltie. He was very nice and gave me a big bagful.'

'I thought you said you only gave

30

Sheltie three,' said Emma.

'Oh, I did,' said Gregory. 'It was a big bag, but there were only three teeny-weeny apples inside.'

Emma realized that Gregory was talking about Mr Crock. She decided to speak to Mr Crock later, to check Gregory's story.

'Can we give Sheltie his breakfast now?' asked Gregory.

'Go on then. Off you go, both of you,' said Mum. 'I'll make a special pizza for lunch in your honour, Gregory. And don't forget, Emma, Mr Thorne is coming early this afternoon and you're not to ride Sheltie yet for at least another day.'

'I know,' said Emma. Though she didn't mean to, she sounded snappy.

31

Emma didn't like to be reminded how to look after Sheltie. But the real reason she was snappy was because she didn't like Gregory feeding Sheltie treats without asking first.

Sheltie was standing by the paddock fence waiting for Emma. But when he saw her, instead of blowing his normal snort, Sheltie gave a loud belch.

'Sheltie!' laughed Emma. 'Manners, please!'

'My father does that,' said Gregory.

'Where is your father?' asked Emma. 'Did he go shopping with your mum?'

'No,' said Gregory. He seemed to be thinking about what to say next. 'Dad's too busy with his work to come on holiday with us. He has to work away a lot. Anyway, it's more fun with just my mother. She lets me do what I like.'

Emma took the key from inside the tack room and unlocked the paddock gate. She hugged Sheltie, then looked down to check his bandage before she gave him his breakfast. The bandage was all wonky and twisted up his leg.

'I tried to straighten it earlier,' said Gregory. 'But I didn't do a very good job, did I?'

Emma didn't like the idea of Gregory touching Sheltie's bandage either, but she didn't say so.

'I'll do it properly,' she said. Then Emma untied the bandage and examined Sheltie's leg.

There was hardly any swelling at all

now. Emma rewrapped Sheltie's leg and the bandage looked smooth and neat.

Then Emma gave Sheltie his measure of pony nuts.

'That's not much, is it?' said Gregory.

'It's plenty,' said Emma in a strict voice. And she watched as Sheltie wolfed down the lot. When he had finished, Sheltie let out another loud belch. Emma chuckled.

'Come on, I'll show you Sheltie's tack, if you like,' she said, 'and how to put it on. But we're not to ride him. We'll take him for a walk and I'll show you Horseshoe Pond and the meadow.'

Gregory was very interested in

Sheltie's saddle and bridle. He told
Emma that he had ridden ponies
before but he had never tacked up on
his own.

Gregory was a fast learner and
Emma had to show him only once
how to do it.

She let Gregory take the saddle and

bridle off again, then fitted Sheltie's
head collar and lead rein.

'Are you ready, boy? Walkies!' said
Emma. But Sheltie didn't seem very
interested at all in going for a walk. He
just dragged behind as Emma led him
out into the lane.

Chapter Five

All through the walk, Sheltie seemed
to have only half the energy he usually
had. And when Emma and Gregory
sat beneath the sycamore tree at
Horseshoe Pond, Sheltie just stood
there with his head low, looking
miserable.

'I don't think Sheltie's feeling very
well,' said Emma.

'Perhaps he's just tired,' said

Gregory. 'His leg looks fine to me.'

'It's not his leg I'm worried about,' snapped Emma. 'He's not very well. I know Sheltie. Something else is wrong. Luckily the vet's coming over this afternoon. I'll ask him. Mr Thorne knows everything about ponies.'

Gregory stared down at his trainers and suddenly went very quiet.

'I don't think I'll come back for lunch after all,' he said.

'You've got to,' said Emma. 'Mum's making pizza especially for you and, anyway, you're supposed to be spending the day. You told your mother you were.'

'But it doesn't really matter, does it?' said Gregory. His face had a funny sneer to it.

All of a sudden, Emma didn't think Gregory was so nice after all.

'I'll walk back with you though,' said Gregory. He switched on his brilliant smile again. 'Then I think I'll go and explore the shops in the village.'

There was nothing Emma could do. After all, she couldn't force Gregory to stay. But she still felt cross all the same. Mum was busy making a special lunch and Gregory wasn't even going to bother to turn up to eat it.

But Emma was more concerned about Sheltie now, and didn't care if Gregory went off on his own or not.

Later though, back at the cottage, Mum was very concerned.

'You shouldn't have let him go off

39

on his own like that, Emma. His mother thinks we're looking after him.'

'I couldn't stop him,' complained Emma sulkily. 'It's not my fault. And I don't like him very much any more either,' she added.

'No, he's not a very thoughtful boy, is he?' said Mum, eyeing the freshly baked pizza.

Dad came in from the garden for lunch and Mum told him what had happened.

'He's a cheeky little thing that Gregory, isn't he?' said Dad. 'But I wouldn't worry too much. There's nothing that can happen to him in Little Applewood. I only hope that the boy learns some manners!'

Mum cut the pizza and they sat
down to eat. Between mouthfuls,
Emma told them about Sheltie.

'Don't worry,' said Mum. 'Mr
Thorne will be calling by soon. He'll
sort Sheltie out.'

When Mr Thorne did arrive, Sheltie
seemed to be worse than ever. He
stood in his field shelter with his head

41

low and looked very sorry for himself.
And as Mr Thorne checked his leg,
Sheltie let out another loud belch.

'He's been doing that all morning,'
said Emma.

Mr Thorne said that Sheltie's leg
was almost better, but was concerned
as to why Sheltie should suddenly be
burping so much.

'Have you changed his diet? Been
feeding him anything different or been
giving him extra treats, Emma?' he
asked.

'No, I haven't,' said Emma.

Mr Thorne pressed Sheltie's tummy
and Sheltie gave a loud whinny as
though he was in pain. Then he
belched again. 'Burrrp!'

'Well, someone has given him

something!' said the vet. 'Poor Sheltie is full of gas.'

Suddenly Emma remembered that Gregory had fed Sheltie some apples earlier that morning. She told Mr Thorne.

'How many apples did he give Sheltie, Emma?' asked Mr Thorne.

Mum joined in the conversation.

'Gregory said he only gave Sheltie three tiny ones, but now I'm beginning to wonder. I shall telephone Mr Crock right now and ask him exactly how many apples were in that bag!'

When Mum came out of the cottage after speaking to Mr Crock, she looked really cross.

Mr Thorne had just finished rewrapping Sheltie's leg, and stood up as Mum said, 'It was a lot more than three apples, I'm afraid. Apparently, Gregory told Mr Crock that I needed apples to bake some pies. Mr Crock thought they were for me and picked Gregory at least ten whoppers from his tree. The worst bit though is that they weren't even eating apples. They were all cookers!'

'Oh dear!' said Mr Thorne. 'And I suppose greedy Sheltie ate the lot? No wonder he's feeling off colour. Sheltie has one big tummy-ache!'

'Just wait till I see that Gregory again,' said Emma crossly. 'I'll make *him* eat ten cooking apples and see if *he* likes it!'

'Gregory probably didn't mean to make Sheltie ill, Emma,' said Mum softly. 'He just didn't think. He's been a very silly boy.' She put her arm around Emma's shoulder and gave her a hug.

'Is there anything we can do to help Sheltie, Mr Thorne?' Mum asked.

'I can give Sheltie an injection to ease the pain, but it's nothing serious. Nature will take its course. Just keep Sheltie walking to help him get rid of the gas. But not outside, Emma. Walk him here in the paddock.'

'Will Sheltie's leg be all right for him to walk a lot?' said Emma.

'Oh yes. Sheltie's leg is fine now,' said Mr Thorne. 'You can take the bandage off tomorrow and perhaps take him for a gentle ride. But no trotting, cantering or galloping.

Walking only for two days.'

After Mr Thorne had gone, Emma began exercising Sheltie. She walked with him in big circles round and round the paddock.

Sheltie was belching all the time now. Some of his burps were really

loud. Emma felt sorry for Sheltie, but she couldn't help giggling. She had never heard Sheltie make these strange noises before.

Later that afternoon, Sheltie was feeling much better. He had got rid of most of the tummy gas and was again interested in everything that went on around him.

'Fancy eating all those apples in one go, Sheltie!' said Emma as she stroked his furry face. 'But it wasn't really your fault, was it? That Gregory should never have given them to you in the first place.'

Now Emma knew why Gregory didn't want to come back to the cottage for pizza. He knew that Mr

Thorne would find out about the apples.

Somehow, Emma didn't think she would be seeing Gregory again. But Emma didn't realize how wrong she was.

Chapter Six

Sunday mornings were always lazy mornings in Emma's house. Everyone slept in a little bit later and took things nice and slowly.

Emma woke to the sound of the church bells. She lay in bed counting the chimes. There were nine.

'Nine!' cried Emma out loud. She sat up quickly.

Emma could hardly believe it. She

never, ever slept in that late. Even on Sundays.

Then she heard Sheltie outside. He seemed to be making a lot of noise this morning. Sheltie was snorting and neighing really loudly.

Emma got up and looked out of the window. What she saw made her gasp in horror. Gregory Blue was out there riding Sheltie bareback – and he wasn't even wearing a hat! He was holding on to Sheltie's mane and making him race round and round the paddock.

Emma couldn't put on her clothes quickly enough. She was in such a hurry that everything went wrong.

First she couldn't find her jeans. And when she did she pulled them on backwards. Then she couldn't find one armhole of her T-shirt and struggled putting it over her head too. And when she couldn't see her boots, she decided not to bother with them at all. Instead, Emma pushed her feet into her fluffy, rabbit slippers and hurried down the stairs.

Emma was yelling at the top of her voice even before she reached the back door.

Mum and Dad flew out of their bedroom to see what all the noise was about.

'Get off him right this minute!' yelled Emma as she tore down the garden.

When Sheltie heard Emma's voice, he stopped in his tracks. And Gregory fell off the little pony.

'Oww!' Gregory bashed his arm as he landed.

Emma didn't care if Gregory was hurt or not. She was more worried about Sheltie. She patted his neck then ran her hand down his bad leg, checking for any swelling. Luckily, there was none.

Gregory leaped to his feet and rubbed his arm. Emma opened her mouth to give Gregory a right telling-off. But to Emma's surprise Gregory just smiled and said, 'Good morning, lazybones.'

Then Emma exploded: 'How dare you ride Sheltie like that! Don't you ever come anywhere near him ever, ever again. Don't you know Sheltie still has a bad leg?'

'It looks all right to me,' said Gregory.

Emma was speechless. By this time Mum and Dad had reached the paddock. They had seen Gregory riding Sheltie and they had also seen him fall off. He had a red mark on his arm just below his shirt sleeve, and would probably have a nasty bruise later.

'Are you all right, Gregory?' asked Mum.

Gregory nodded.

'That was very thoughtless of you, riding Sheltie like that.' Mum sounded very stern. 'You could have made Sheltie's leg worse.'

'And did you realize that you made Sheltie feel very ill by giving him all those apples?' added Dad.

Gregory suddenly took everyone by surprise and burst into tears.

'Sorry, Sheltie,' he sobbed, then he ran away out of the paddock and down the lane.

Chapter Seven

Emma, Mum and Dad just stood there and watched him disappear. Suddenly they all felt really awful. One minute they were annoyed with Gregory and now they felt sorry for him, even though it was Gregory who had been naughty.

Sheltie blew a raspberry to remind everyone that he was still there. Then he gave a snort and nudged Emma as if to say, 'I'm OK, really!'

Emma gave his neck a hug and buried her face in his bushy mane.

'Come on, boy,' she said. 'Breakfast time.'

For the rest of the day, Emma kept thinking about Gregory. Although he had been naughty, Emma didn't think that Gregory had really meant any harm. He was just a silly boy who did things without thinking first.

Now he's spoilt everything, she thought. We could have been friends.

In the afternoon, when Emma checked Sheltie's bandage again, there was still no swelling at all. Sheltie's leg was much better and he was standing comfortably on all fours. He was even prancing on the spot and being quite frisky.

Emma left the bandage off but decided not to ride Sheltie until the following day. Instead, she took Sheltie out for another walk and found herself leading him down the lane towards the cottage Gregory was staying at.

Emma wondered if they would see Gregory. She felt bad about yelling at him. Emma remembered how upset Gregory had been and she was sorry that she had made him cry.

At Stepps Cottage, Emma stopped for a minute and let Sheltie crop the grass growing against the cottage wall. She looked up at the windows but she couldn't see anyone. Sheltie looked up too.

Then the front door swung open
and a woman stepped out. Emma
realized it must be Gregory's mother.
She stared first at Emma and then at
Sheltie. She didn't look very friendly
at all.

'Hello,' said Emma cheerfully. 'This
is Sheltie and my name's Emma. We
live just down the lane.'

Gregory's mother scowled. 'I
guessed it must be you,' she said.
'What are you doing out with that
dangerous animal?'

Emma was taken completely by
surprise. Sheltie tossed his head and
gave a friendly blow.

'He's not dangerous!' said Emma.
'Sheltie is as gentle as a lamb. He
wouldn't hurt a fly.'

'Well, that's not what I've heard,' snapped Gregory's mother. 'That animal has kicked and bitten my Gregory. It ought to be locked up out of harm's way. I've a good mind to call the police right now and have it taken away!'

Emma couldn't believe her ears. She didn't know what to say. Emma just stood there with her mouth hanging open.

Mrs Blue carried on, 'My Gregory's arm is all bruised. And that animal did it.' She pointed an accusing finger as she spoke and jabbed the air towards Sheltie.

Sheltie didn't like being pointed at and flattened his ears. Then, suddenly, Emma found her voice.

'Sheltie didn't kick or bite Gregory,' she said. 'Sheltie would never do a thing like that! Gregory was riding Sheltie without asking and fell off. I saw it myself. Why don't you ask him?'

But Gregory's mother wouldn't listen.

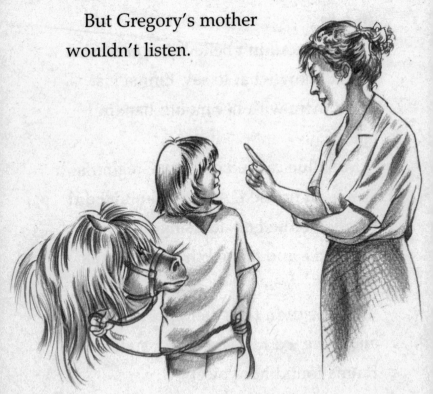

'Take that pony and stay away,' she said crossly. Then she stepped back inside and slammed the door.

Emma saw Gregory's face appear at an upstairs window. But when Gregory saw Emma looking up, he ducked away out of sight.

'Come on, Sheltie,' said Emma. 'Let's go back home.' She turned Sheltie and walked him back down the lane to his paddock.

'What nasty people,' thought Emma. She would be glad when Gregory and his mother went back home to wherever they came from!

Chapter Eight

The next day, when Emma got home
from school, she ran to the paddock
to see Sheltie. But Emma's little pony
was nowhere to be seen.

The gate was bolted and the
padlock was hanging in place. But the
key was still in it. Emma would never
have left it like that!

Emma shivered with panic. She ran
to check the field shelter, but Sheltie

wasn't there. Sheltie had gone.

Emma raced to the tack room.
Inside, she found that Sheltie's saddle
and bridle had gone too! Someone
had taken them, as well as Sheltie.

All of a sudden Emma felt really
angry. She could think of only one
person who would do such a thing:
Gregory Blue.

Emma ran into the cottage, yelling
at the top of her voice.

Mum was busy in her little office,
writing letters. Emma came bursting
in and told her as quickly as she
could what had happened. She was
so upset she could hardly breathe.

'It's that Gregory!' she cried. 'I
know it is. He's taken Sheltie out
riding.'

'Now calm down, Emma,' said Mum. 'We don't know for certain that it is Gregory.'

But Emma couldn't think of anyone else who would have come to the cottage, tacked up Sheltie and taken him away.

'First things first,' announced Mum. 'We'll go down to Stepps Cottage right now and see if Gregory is there. He may have just taken Sheltie to show his mother.'

'I don't think so,' said Emma. 'She hates Sheltie!'

They fetched Joshua, who had been quietly watching TV, and started to walk down the lane. Emma hurried ahead.

'Wait for us, Emma,' said Mum. She

picked up Joshua and quickened her pace.

Emma was already at Stepps Cottage and banging on the front door as Mum caught up. It seemed to take ages before anyone answered, but finally the door opened and Mrs Blue stood on the front step looking puzzled.

'Where's Sheltie?' demanded Emma. 'He's gone missing. Has Gregory got him?'

'Now hold on, young lady,' said Mrs Blue. It was clear that she didn't like Emma's tone of voice.

Mum stepped in and explained what had been happening over the past few days.

'I'm afraid Gregory has been telling silly lies to everyone,' said Mum. 'Especially about Sheltie biting and kicking him. Gregory was riding Sheltie without permission and he fell off.'

'Oh dear!' exclaimed Mrs Blue, looking a little embarrassed. 'Gregory said that he'd spent most of the time exploring the village on his own.'

'I'm afraid that's another lie,' said Mum. 'He's been to visit us quite a few times already.'

Mrs Blue looked very concerned.

'I'm sorry for all the trouble Gregory has caused,' she said. 'He's a nice boy really, but since his father and I got divorced he's been so naughty and tells fibs all the time. He doesn't mean to, but he keeps getting into trouble. That's why I brought him down here for a holiday. I thought a week in the countryside would do him some good and stop his silly pranks.'

Now Mrs Blue looked really worried and upset. 'Gregory went out ages ago,' she said. 'He told me he was going into the village, but I suppose he must have taken Sheltie out for a ride, just like you say. Where on earth could they have gone? I do hope they are both all right!'

'So do I,' said Emma. She had calmed down now. She felt very sorry to hear that Gregory's mum and dad were divorced. Emma remembered Gregory saying that his father worked away a lot. But Gregory didn't say that his father lived away too! Emma thought how awful it would be if her own dad went away.

They all stood there, not really knowing what to do next.

'They could have gone across the downs,' suggested Mum. 'Or through the woods. There are so many places to look.'

Then Mrs Blue remembered

something Gregory had said earlier in the day.

'He was talking about the stream,' she said. 'The one that runs through Little Applewood. Gregory mentioned that he wanted to explore the path of the stream and find out where it started.'

'That's up at Tarr Point,' said Emma. 'Behind the woods, where the stream bubbles up through the rocks. I hope

Gregory hasn't taken Sheltie up there! It's rocky and slippery and very dangerous.'

'Well, we've got to start looking somewhere,' said Mum. 'And there's a footpath that follows the stream up to the Point.'

Emma was deep in thought. 'You don't think anyone else has taken Sheltie, do you, Mum?' She was hoping now that it *was* Gregory, because that meant Sheltie had only been borrowed and not stolen. And although it was dangerous up at the Point, at least Gregory could ride.

'I have a feeling that it is Gregory,' said Mum. 'Let's just hope that he has enough sense to keep Sheltie off the slippery rocks at the top.'

'Let's go then,' said Mrs Blue. 'I'll come with you. It sounds as though we don't have a minute to lose.'

'I think it might be best if you stayed here,' said Mum, 'just in case Gregory comes back. Someone's got to be here. I'd be grateful if you could keep Joshua with you too.'

'Yes, of course, I suppose you're right,' said Mrs Blue. And Emma could see that she was very worried indeed.

Chapter Nine

Emma and Mum set off down the lane. Soon they were crossing the little stone bridge and walking the long footpath up to Tarr Point.

Emma hurried ahead. The sun was setting and the sky had begun to turn red. Emma began thinking of all the terrible things that could have happened to Sheltie.

First she was worried about Sheltie

being ridden with a sore leg. Then she was worried that Gregory might lead Sheltie into danger. The pathway up to the Point was not a proper bridle path. It was full of tree roots and holes that could be dangerous for a little pony.

Emma was also worried about Tarr Point itself. Where the stream began, the water bubbled up out of the sloping rocks. The rocks were smooth and very slippery in places.

Emma couldn't bear to think what might happen if Gregory took Sheltie on to those sloping rocks. The idea of Sheltie slipping and falling was horrible.

Emma suddenly realized that tears were running down her cheeks. She wiped them away with her sleeve and took a deep breath.

'Please let Sheltie be all right,'
Emma said out loud. 'Please don't let
anything happen to him.'

Mum gave Emma's hand a
reassuring squeeze. They continued on
the pathway as it climbed up steadily
through the woods. The little stream
bubbled past them on its way down to
Little Applewood. And as they
climbed, the sky above their heads
turned a fiery red.

Emma's legs were beginning to
ache, when suddenly, up ahead, she
heard a familiar sound. It was very
faint, but it was a pony whinnying.

It seemed to be coming from high in
the trees. It was Sheltie calling. Emma
would have recognized his sound

anywhere. She spun round to look at
Mum. Mum had heard it too.

'Sheltie!' Emma said.

Twenty metres in front of them, up
on a higher footpath, was Sheltie. He
was trotting along on his own, looking
for a way down. But there was no sign
of Gregory.

When Sheltie saw Emma he blew a

series of loud snorts and looked over the edge on to the lower path.

'Don't move, Sheltie,' called Emma. 'Stay exactly where you are.' She knew it was safer for her to find a way up to Sheltie than for Sheltie to look for a way down.

But Sheltie couldn't wait. As Emma ran along, searching for a track which joined the two paths, Sheltie trotted along too. He followed Emma's movements up on the higher path. And when Emma did spot the track she was looking for, Sheltie slid down it before Emma had a chance to stop him.

As they met at the bottom, Sheltie pushed his soft muzzle into her chest and Emma threw her arms around his head and kissed his ears. She was so happy to have him back safe and sound.

Sheltie was also pleased to see Emma. And as she hugged him he made soft little pony noises and blew hot breaths down her neck.

'But where is Gregory?' said Mum. There was no sign of the boy anywhere.

Emma held Sheltie's bridle at arm's length and quickly checked him over. His leg seemed fine. But she did notice that his legs were all wet. And he had very muddy hoofs.

Emma called out, 'Gregory! Gregory!' But her voice was lost in the trees. And no one answered.

'He can't be far,' said Mum. 'We're

almost at the top of Tarr Point now. Gregory must have left Sheltie for a moment and Sheltie wandered off.'

'I don't think so,' said Emma. 'I think something has happened. Something terrible.'

Emma looked at Mum. Then she turned to Sheltie and whispered in his ear. 'Where is he? Where's Gregory? You know, boy, don't you? What's happened to him?'

'Do you know where Gregory is, Sheltie?' asked Mum.

Sheltie pawed the ground, then jangled his bit. He definitely seemed to be trying to tell them something.

Emma knew exactly what Sheltie was trying to say. 'He wants us to follow him.'

Emma tucked Sheltie's reins into his bridle. 'Go on, boy. Take us to Gregory.'

Sheltie turned and trotted away up the path. Ten metres along he stopped and looked back. When he saw they

were following, Sheltie carried on.

They followed the little Shetland pony all the way to the top of Tarr Point, where the path opened up on to flatter ground, and the soft grass turned to hard rock. Every step of the way they kept a lookout for any signs of Gregory.

They kept calling his name, but there was no answer.

When they reached the Point itself, they saw the source of the stream bubbling up through the flat, smooth rocks. And there, lying in a heap in the middle of the water, was Gregory's sweatshirt.

Before Emma could stop him, Sheltie rushed forward and stepped out on to the flat, slippery rock.

'Come back,' called Emma. But Sheltie slowly inched his way forward. Then he bent his head low to pick up Gregory's sweatshirt between his teeth.

And he slipped.

Emma gasped in horror as Sheltie slid down the sloping rock and stumbled on to a very narrow ledge. Sheltie was in real trouble. A steep drop fell away below on one side. And the dangerous, slippery rocks rose before him on the other. There seemed to be no way out!

Sheltie stood on the narrow ledge and looked back up at Emma. Then he made a frightened snort and Emma burst into tears.

Chapter Ten

Suddenly, Gregory appeared from behind a large rock and Emma could see a nasty graze on his forehead. All his clothes were soaking wet. He had seen what had happened and gave a weak, nervous smile.

'I'm sorry,' he said. 'I'm really, truly sorry. Sheltie's in trouble and it's all my fault.' He used the back of his hand to wipe the tears from his eyes.

'I tried to take Sheltie across the stream and on to the rocks, but he wouldn't go. So I left him and went on foot. Then I slipped and fell!'

Gregory continued, 'Sheltie came to my rescue. He pulled me up out of the water. And now he's stuck on that ledge and it's all my fault!'

Emma was listening to Gregory, but she couldn't take her eyes off Sheltie.

'I've got to go and get him,' she said.

'No!' cried Mum. She caught hold of Emma's arm. 'It's far too dangerous. We'll have to go back to the village for help!'

But before Mum could say any more, Gregory had stepped out on to the slippery rocks to try to save Sheltie.

'Stop! Gregory, come back,' Emma called.

But it was too late. Gregory was already edging his way down Tarr Point to reach Sheltie. Emma held her breath and watched as Gregory inched his way across the wet, sloping rock.

Sheltie saw him coming. He didn't move his legs but raised his head slowly and blew a sad whicker as if to say, 'Help!'

'Don't worry, Sheltie. I'm coming,' said Gregory.

'Be careful,' called Emma. She could hardly bear to watch. Mum gasped as Gregory missed his footing and slipped down on to the same ledge as Sheltie.

Sheltie gently nuzzled Gregory's hand.

'Good boy, Sheltie,' Gregory said soothingly. 'I'll soon have you out of here.' He stroked Sheltie's face and spoke gently. Sheltie seemed very pleased that Gregory was there.

'How are they going to get back up?' said Emma. 'He'll never be able to lead Sheltie up that rocky slope.'

Emma felt as though her tummy was tying itself in knots. Any minute now she expected Sheltie to fall right off the edge.

Then, much to Emma and Mum's surprise, Gregory began urging Sheltie to walk backwards along the narrow rock.

'What's he doing?' cried Emma. 'There's nowhere to go behind them. They'll fall off!' And there was nothing they could do but stand there and watch.

Gregory continued to urge Sheltie backwards and Sheltie seemed quite happy to trust him.

What Emma and Mum couldn't see was that, hidden behind Sheltie, the narrow ledge opened up behind a square slab of rock on to a much wider platform.

And the slope back up to the Point from there wasn't half as steep.

'Where have they gone?' yelled Emma as Gregory and Sheltie completely disappeared from view. 'They've fallen off! They must have! Sheltie!'

Then, with a loud whinny and a clattering of hoofs, Sheltie appeared back on the top of the Point, with Gregory holding his reins.

'Sheltie!' cried Emma. Her heart wouldn't stop banging in her chest. She wanted to rush across to him, but Mum held her back.

'Those rocks are still very slippery, Emma,' she said. Mum called to Gregory to be careful as he led Sheltie safely through the stream and across to where Emma stood.

Emma ran to Sheltie and buried her face in his mane. She hugged him and hugged him. 'Oh, Sheltie. You're safe.' Then she looked at Gregory, who was standing there looking very uncomfortable.

'Thank you for saving Sheltie,' she said.

'It was nothing,' said Gregory. 'It was the least I could do. And I'm sorry for putting Sheltie in danger. Sometimes I just don't think. But I've learned my lesson today. I promise I'll never do anything so silly again.'

Emma put her arm around Gregory. 'You were very brave,' she said. 'And I can't thank you enough. But how did you know where that ledge went to?

And why were you hiding behind that rock?'

'Before you came,' said Gregory, 'I had a look around. Then when you started calling and Sheltie ran off I got scared and hid. I knew everyone would be angry with me and I didn't know what to do.'

'Well, it's a good job you did what you did,' said Mum. She was so relieved that everything had turned out as it had and everyone was safe. 'But it was wrong to take Sheltie,' she added.

'I know,' said Gregory. He looked really sorry.

'Come on,' said Mum. 'We'd better start making our way back. Your mother must be so worried.' Then she noticed that Gregory was holding his head.

'Are you all right, Gregory? You've got a nasty bump there!' said Mum.

Gregory said he was feeling tired and his legs had gone wobbly, so they helped him into Sheltie's saddle and Emma led them back down along the path to the village.

Back at Stepps Cottage, Gregory was put straight to bed. Then Mrs Blue

called the doctor. She was so relieved to
have Gregory back home.

Gregory's head turned out to be
nothing serious. Just a nasty bump. But
he had to rest for a day or two.

At the end of the week, Gregory was
back to his bright, cheerful self. He
wandered down to Emma's cottage
with a big sticking plaster across his
forehead. Emma was out in the
paddock with Sheltie.

'I just wanted to come and say
goodbye,' he said. 'It was wrong of me
to take Sheltie without asking. And I'm
really sorry that I made you worry.'

Gregory looked down at his shoes
and his face blushed red.

Emma ruffled Sheltie's mane.

'Well, there was no real harm done, I suppose,' she said. 'But you must promise never to do anything like that again!'

'I won't,' said Gregory. 'I promise. I've really learned my lesson. And can I write to you?' he added quickly.

It was Emma's turn to blush now. After everything that had happened, she still liked Gregory Blue.

'Of course you can,' she said. 'We'd both like that, wouldn't we, Sheltie?'

Sheltie pushed his head forward over the fence and let out a loud belch.

'Sheltie! Manners, please,' said Emma. And as she and Gregory laughed, all the events of the past few days were forgotten.